D0118814

Bayberry & Beau

Illustrations by Gillian Tyler

Bayberry & Beau

BY

Nita Choukas

Chelsea Green Publishing Company
White River Junction, Vermont

Copyright © 2006 by Nita Choukas
Illustrations © 2006 by Gillian Tyler

No part of this book may be transmitted or reproduced in any form
by any means without permission from the publisher.

The text of this book is composed in Goudy, with the display set in
Adobe Garamond and Ares Dee HW.

Book design and composition by Fred Lee

Printed in the United States
First printing, July 2006
10 9 8 7 6 5 4 3 2 1

Cataloging-in-Publication Data is available from the Library of Congress.
ISBN-10: 1-933392-35-5
ISBN-13: 978-1-933392-35-6

Chelsea Green Publishing Company
Post Office Box 428
White River Junction, VT 05001
(800) 639-4099
www.chelseagreen.com

Dedication

To Michael and our children and grandchildren
who believed in me

With Grateful Thanks to:

My friends Margaret and Richard Price, for introducing me to their horse, which led to the inspiration to write *Bayberry and Beau*. I am deeply grateful for their kindness and patience.

Dorothy and Kenneth Purdy, for always welcoming me to their New Hampshire farm to observe their wondrous barn cat and Bayberry. Both the Purdys' and the Prices' understanding and love of animals were models for me.

Nardi Reeder Campion, Joni B. Cole, and Sheila Harvey Tanzer, friends and writers whose criticism and encouragement informed and sustained me.

Fred Lee, for his guidance, talents and his abiding friendship.

And by no means least, my daughters, author Melanie Choukas-Bradley, writer Eleanor Anderson, and my son, Michael, who read a seemingly endless number of revisions, and my husband, Mike, who not only read but typed each page, and whose support throughout this undertaking kept me going.

Bayberry
&
Beau

1

Beau was having a wonderful dream. He wasn't a barn cat anymore. He was just Miki's pet again, sleeping on the bottom of his bed.

In his dream, Miki was poking him. "Wake up, Beau, wake up and play with me."

Beau opened his eyes. Miki wasn't there. He wasn't on Miki's bed. He was still in the hayloft above the horse stable on Cloudland Farm. He looked around thinking, "This isn't where I want to be. I want to be in Miki's house."

Then Beau remembered what he was supposed to be doing instead of sleeping in the loft. "Man, Jake is going to scold me again for sacking out all night instead of doing my job—catching mice." Beau shuddered at the thought of doing such a thing.

"Maybe tomorrow night I will catch a mouse, but not now." Beau curled up into a ball, tucking his head under his yellow striped fur for another snooze.

Back at Miki's house that same night, Miki's coughing had awakened Mother. Quickly getting out of bed, she wrapped her robe around her and hurried down the hallway to his bedroom.

"Mom is here, dear," she said, turning on his bedside lamp. Miki was sitting up in bed, struggling for breath between coughs. His shoulders were hunched, and his eyes were wide and anxious. He was having an asthma attack.

Kneeling beside his bed, Mother plumped his pillows into a backrest and straightened up his small body to make breathing easier. She felt his forehead. It was warm with fever.

Plugging in the vaporizer always kept at his bedside, Mother explained she would be right back with his medicine.

"Are you ready for the bad-tasting one first, dear?" asked Mother when she returned carrying a small tray.

"Yup."

Miki shivered as he swallowed, but he knew the sweet-tasting cough syrup that came next would wash away the bitter taste on his tongue.

Mother gently smoothed vapor rub on his chest, and the little dab she put under his nose made breathing seem easier. She pulled a chair next to his bed and supported him in an upright position with her right arm and held his left hand in hers. The gurgling vaporizer and Miki's wheezing were the only sounds in the room as they both dozed between Miki's coughing spells.

As the medicine began to work, Miki talked a little between naps. "Mom, how come I still get asthma when Beau doesn't even live here anymore?"

"Remember Dr. Woodleton explaining that the bad germs that give you colds give you asthma too?"

"Well, I wish the germs would go away like Beau had to."

"So do I, dear."

"I miss Beau so much, Mom,"

"I know you do, Miki. We all do. It's sad that he can't live with us anymore."

"Probably if I outgrow my asthma, he can come back, right?"

"Right, dear. But now I don't think you should talk anymore. Try to close your eyes and rest."

Miki closed his eyes. Mother sat silently watching the steam encircling his flushed face, curling his long lashes. When he dozed in less labored breathing, he looked like a cherub.

In his sleep, Miki was dreaming he was chasing Beau in a large, green meadow. Every time he got close enough to catch him in his arms, Beau disappeared. Miki would sink to the ground in disappointment, then Beau would go running by him again. Each time, when he almost caught him, Beau vanished.

"Wait, Beau, wait!" Miki called in his sleep. Mother gently awakened him. "I couldn't catch Beau, Mom."

"It was just a dream, dear. Go back to sleep, and just as soon as you are better, we'll go see Beau at Aunt Ruby's and Uncle Jake's house."

"Good." Miki smiled and closed his eyes.

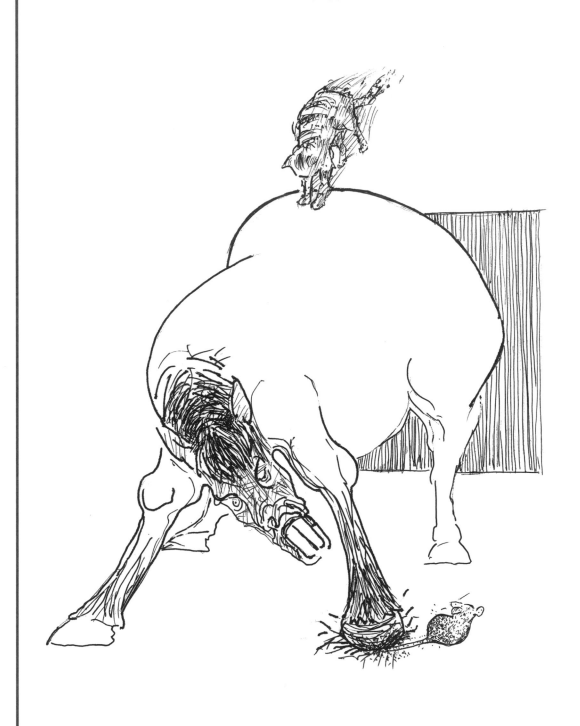

2

As Beau lay sleeping in the loft, in the stable below, Marvin, a small mouse with gray velvet fur, poked his nose out of his mouse hole in the feed room.

"Good, Jake hasn't come down from the farmhouse yet to feed the horses," he thought.

Scurrying across the feed room floor, Marvin squeezed under the door to the stable. He looked left. He looked right. Beau was nowhere in sight.

"Ha, that cat's too lazy to be up this early."

Marvin crept from stall to stall, peeking to see if any of the barn's seven horses had left scattered grain from last night's supper.

"Durn, some dude got up earlier than I did and licked every floor clean."

Disappointed, the hungry mouse sat resting his chin on his front paws to think. There was one stall left to check out: Sure Bett's.

Sure Bett, a rather mean Morgan mare, hated mice. They were all afraid to sneak grain from her stall.

"Should I take a chance and creep into Sure Bett's stall?" Marvin wondered.

Marvin was so hungry his stomach ached. With a thumping heart and twitching whiskers he crawled toward Bett's stall. She was sleeping standing up, the way she usually napped. He could see grain scattered around her feed bucket.

Marvin pushed his snout further through the knothole to be sure Bett was still asleep. He couldn't see that Bett's eyes were barely open, just enough for her to see his whiskers poking through the hole. When she saw them, she closed her eyes tight to trick him.

"Yup, Bett's fast asleep. I'll be quiet and quick. My stomach is so empty I need to eat," thought Marvin.

Marvin crept toward the scattered grain. He ate as fast as he could, not knowing Sure Bett was watching him. When his stomach was full, he grabbed a final mouthful to carry back to his mate, Mattie. He crawled as fast as he could out of Bett's stall. He didn't make it.

In a flash, Sure Bett's hoof stomped on his tail, pinning him to the cement floor.

"Eek, eek!" Marvin's pitiful squealing rang through the stable. All the other mice trembled in their holes. They knew something terrible must be happening to him. They huddled around Mattie, trying to comfort her.

The trapped Marvin wriggled desperately to free himself.

"You creepy little thief, Marvin. I've warned you to keep away from my grain bucket," snapped Bett.

The loud squeals and scolding awakened Beau from his cat nap above in the loft.

Yawning and stretching himself awake, Beau crept to the edge of the loft and peered down on Sure Bett's stall. His sleepy yellow eyes widened in horror when he saw Marvin's tail under Sure Bett's hoof.

Beau didn't know what to do. Being the only barn cat on Cloudland Farm, it was his job to get rid of mice, not save them.

But Beau could not bear to see Marvin in pain. He had to outwit Sure Bett somehow. Thinking fast, he called down to her.

"Sure Bett, I'll be right down to get rid of that pesky mouse for you."

Looking up at him, Bett snorted and scoffed at Beau's offer.

"You can't catch a mouse, Beau, not even a trapped one. We

all know what a coward you are."

"I am not a coward. I'm coming right down to help you." Beau hurried down the ladder and surprised Bett with his speedy arrival on her stall door.

"Okay, Bett. You lift your hoof, and I'll grab the mouse and get him out of here," instructed Beau.

Bett had a way of curling her lips around her big front teeth that made her look ridiculous.

"I don't trust you, Beau. My hoof is staying right where it is."

"Okay. I'll jump on him first, grab him in my claws, and when you know I have him, you can lift your hoof. Here goes," said Beau.

Beau took a flying leap through the air, but he sailed straight for the horse, not the mouse. He landed on Sure Bett's back with his sharp claws digging into her hide. The surprised mare reared at the attack on her back, freeing Marvin from under her hoof.

"Run, Marvin, run!" shouted Beau, jumping from Bett's back to the floor next to Marvin.

"Get up, Marvin! Get up and run!" Bett was ready to stomp on him again.

Beau jumped to safety on the stall door. "Hurry before Sure Bett traps you again, Marvin," yelled Beau.

Marvin's fear gave him the energy to struggle to his feet and crawl to safety just in time. Furious because she had been tricked, Sure Bett started kicking the wall of her stall.

Marvin and Beau were exhausted from their ordeal. Marvin was licking his tail, and Beau was hunched up on the stable floor, resting before climbing back to the loft.

"Go back to your hole, Marvin, and don't ever go near Bett's stall again," said Beau in a quivering voice.

Marvin looked at Beau with his tiny beady eyes. "Why don't you want to catch me, Beau?" Beau was embarrassed. He didn't answer Marvin.

"Just go back to your hole before I do," snapped Beau.

"You were very brave to save me, Beau," said Marvin.

No one had ever called Beau brave before. He stared at the little mouse.

"You—you really think I was brave, Marvin?"

"Yes, I do, Beau. Sure Bett could have hurt you, too."

Beau sat up and looked directly into Marvin's eyes, suddenly feeling confident.

"Well, Marvin, don't ever go into Bett's stall again. Next time you may not escape. Man, I'm tired. It was hard work saving you, Marvin, but you know what I'm supposed to do to you, don't you?"

Marvin shivered as he said very softly, "Yes."

Beau watched Marvin crawling slowly back to the feed room, dragging his sore tail behind him. Then he climbed the ladder to the loft. Before lying down for a nap, he looked down on Sure Bett's stall.

The angry mare was looking up at him. Her teeth looked huge when she threatened him. "I'll get even with you, Beau."

3

It was not a peaceful morning up the hill in the farmhouse kitchen, either. Ruby was scolding her husband Jake.

"Jake, that useless Beau has to go. What sense is there in keeping a barn cat that doesn't hunt?"

"Now, Ruby."

"Don't you 'Now, Ruby' me. You know the mice are getting out of control around here. Every time I go down to the stable, I see them scurrying across the floor. I don' t know why that cat isn't starving. Lord knows I don't give him enough scraps to live on."

As Ruby sputtered, Jake sat silently eating his oatmeal.

Setting Jake's cocoa and toast on the table, Ruby spoke less sharply.

"The new neighbors up the road said they'd take Beau off our hands and give him to their grandson for his birthday. He has been teasing his parents for a pet. Then we could get another cat—a real barn cat—to get rid of the mice."

Jake sat upright in his chair. "Now don't you go giving Beau away, Ruby. You know it would break Miki's heart if he couldn't see Beau when he comes here. Beau is still Miki's pet even though he can't live in his house. He's not yours to give away."

Ruby pressed her hands on the table and looked squarely into Jake's eyes.

"Jake, when are you going to start running this farm with your head instead of your heart?"

After a long pause, Jake spoke slowly. "Ruby, I run this farm by working hard seven days a week."

"I know how hard you work, Jake. That's why I am so upset that you agreed to take in that old horse, Bayberry, to board. You don't need a horse who is blind in one eye and allergic to hay, of all things. What are we becoming—a home for useless animals?"

Jake pushed his chair away from the table. He was too upset to finish his breakfast.

"I told you, Ruby, that Doc Pringle is going to examine Bayberry thoroughly when she arrives. If he thinks she will be too much trouble for us, I will tell her owners, Peggy and Dick, to find another place to board their horse."

Jake grabbed his cap from a hook by the door. He let the screen door slam behind him and headed down the hill to feed the horses.

Breathing the air of the early June morning soothed him. The smell of freshly plowed soil from Ruby's vegetable garden raised his spirits. He admired the artistic way Ruby had planted the dwarf fruit trees in the orchard below the garden.

"Ruby's great at planting and cooking," he thought. "I just wish she wasn't so good at telling me what she thinks."

Jake stopped to scan the emerald fields that stretched to a distant tree line backed by a hazy purple mountain ridge. Oxeye daisies quivered in the light breeze blowing across the hay meadow.

All around him the countryside was bursting with the freshness of a new growing season.

A bluebird warbled from a branch of the crab apple tree. A cardinal whistled. Jake whistled back to him.

"Ah, June is my favorite month on Cloudland Farm," he thought, hurrying down the hill.

Jake slid the stable door open. The horses nickered friendly greetings, except for Sure Bett, who snorted at him.

"Sorry I'm late, my friends. Chow's coming right up." Jake

opened the feed room door. Two mice scampered from sight.

"Ruby's right. The mice are getting out of control. I have a problem—a big one. Oh well," he thought, "I'll think about that later."

Whistling his worry away, Jake gathered grain and went to feed Sure Bett first.

"Good morning, beautiful Bett." Sure Bett began eating without looking at Jake. Shaking his head, Jake spoke softly to her. "What a mystery your misery is to me, Bett. You have the body of a champion, but you don't have the soul of one. I wish I knew how to help you."

After feeding the other horses, Jake went to look for Beau. Clapping his hands, he called up to the loft. "Come on down, Beau. I know you are up there."

Jake's voice in the morning meant breakfast for Beau too. The cat hurried down the ladder and ran to Jake, rubbing and purring against his legs.

Jake scooped Beau into his arms. "Beau, if you don't start hunting instead of sleeping all night, Ruby is going to send you away and get another barn cat. If that happens, you won't see Miki every Saturday when he comes to visit us."

Jake held Beau close to his chest and scratched behind his ears. "I know you don't like being a barn cat, fella. You would rather still be living in Miki's house, playing with him and sleeping at the bottom of his bed, wouldn't you? Miki misses you too, Beau."

Jake carried Beau to the feed room. Looking at Jake, Beau's large yellow eyes narrowed with contentment at being held, being talked to.

Setting Beau down, Jake opened a cupboard door and reached far back to pull a bag of cat food from its hiding place. He filled an old tin pie plate to the brim with nuggets.

"If Ruby finds out I'm buying cat food for you, Beau, we'll both be in trouble."

Watching Jake intently, Beau tipped his head to one side. "He knows what I'm saying to him," thought Jake.

Jake crouched beside Beau, watching him hungrily grabbing mouthfuls of cat food. He loved the throaty purring sound Beau made when he was eating. Jake's blue eyes twinkled, his smile lines crinkled. He ran his palm along Beau's back.

"I'll leave you in peace, Beau. I hear Sure Bett fussing. She's finished eating and wants to go outside."

Jake led the horses from the darkness of the stable into the bright June morning. "Go get the goodies, my friends, but leave some for Bayberry. She'll be coming to keep you company very soon."

4

Many miles south of Cloudland Farm in New Hampshire, Bayberry was waking in her barn in Connecticut. Her owners, Peggy and Dick, had already filled her grain bucket and left her stall door open so she could trot up the hill to the school bus stop.

In all kinds of weather, Bayberry faithfully saw the neighborhood children off to school in the morning and welcomed them home in the afternoon.

Climbing a hill was not easy for the old horse, especially in the morning when her joints were stiff and it hurt her to walk fast. Midway up the hill she stopped to rest. Her ears perked. Voices were drifting down the hill.

"Good, the bus hasn't come yet," she thought.

The children were waiting and watching for Bayberry's head to poke over the crest of the hill. They shrieked when they saw her.

"Here she comes! Here she comes!"

Like a flock of birds taking flight, they flew to meet their faithful friend. Clutching clumps of wildflowers they had picked for her, the children clustered around Bayberry, arguing over whose turn it was to feed her first. It didn't matter to the hungry horse. She gently took a bite from the closest hand.

The insistent beeping of the school bus horn ended the feeding fracas. The bus driver didn't mind beeping several times. She liked Bayberry, too.

After the bus left, Bayberry ate the flowers thrown on the ground for her, then lifted her head to sniff the air for cooking smells that might be floating from a neighbor's kitchen window.

"Corn bread. I smell corn bread."

The tempting smell was coming from Fran's house across the road from the bus stop. Before crossing, she waited for a trailer truck to pass. Large trucks seldom traveled on the country road that wound through the neighborhood. Bayberry stopped to watch its snaky motion going down the hill. She was surprised when the truck slowed and turned into her driveway.

Her curiosity was stronger than her appetite for corn bread, and she headed home to see what was happening.

Dick, her owner, was in the driveway talking to two men. He shook hands with them, and the strangers followed Dick into the house.

Bayberry circled the truck, sniffing the tires. She wondered if it was a huge horse trailer.

Peggy came out of the barn carrying Bayberry's saddle. She was surprised to see her horse by the moving van.

"Bayberry, why are you back so soon? Wasn't there anything good cooking in the neighborhood?"

Eyeing her saddle in Peggy's hand, Bayberry nickered and trotted toward her in excitement.

"Peggy's taking me for a trail ride," she thought.

Peggy knew immediately what Bayberry was thinking. She dropped the saddle next to the box of Bayberry's blankets and brushes that she had packed for the move to their new retirement home in New Hampshire. Their Connecticut farm was too much to care for as she and Dick grew older.

"No, girl, we aren't going on a trail ride today. Tomorrow Dick and I are going to take you for a long ride in your trailer to New Hampshire. There will be lots of time there for us to explore new trails together. Tomorrow is moving day, Bayberry."

The next morning Peggy was watching Bayberry eating her last breakfast in her Connecticut barn.

She had filled her grain bucket before daylight. Dick was up early, too, checking the horse trailer to be sure all the padding was in place for the long ride to Cloudland Farm.

Chewing her grain, Bayberry stared at Peggy. Peggy's pretty round face and lively eyes looked sad.

"Peggy doesn't want to go to New Hampshire, either," thought Bayberry.

Peggy was struggling to keep from crying. She pressed her cheek against Bayberry's muzzle. She was remembering a day long ago—their daughter Wendy's eighth birthday. Though twenty-three years had passed, Peggy remembered the look of joy on Wendy's face when she first saw her birthday present, a four-year-old bay quarterhorse with friendly brown eyes.

Peggy's thoughts recalled the years of watching the little girl and the horse working long hours together to prepare for competition in horse shows.

She smiled remembering the happy years of the championship seasons that followed—Wendy riding Bayberry into the winner's circle time after time.

Shouting in the dooryard startled Peggy from her reverie. A chorus of children's voices rang out, "Surprise! Surprise!"

Peggy led Bayberry into the early morning light to find all the neighbors clustered around Dick, and the neighborhood children were coming toward them. Little Esther, the youngest child, was carrying a garland of red clover.

"We made this for Bayberry," she said proudly, handing it to Peggy.

"Oh, red clover is Bayberry's favorite treat. Thank you so much, everybody." Bayberry sniffed at the garland, and while Peggy was talking, she took a huge bite out of it. This brought shrieks of laughter from the children.

"She likes it! She likes it!" cried Esther.

Fran, the next-door neighbor, called the group to attention. She had a large decorated basket filled with wrapped packages. "We know you are eager to get on your way to New Hampshire, Peg and Dick, but we wanted to say one last good-bye. We collected a few things that will help tide you over until you have a chance to shop, Peg." Fran's voice quavered. She had to pause before finishing what she had to say.

"We're going to miss you, Peggy and Dick, and life won't be the same without Bayberry grazing in our yards and coming to peek in our kitchen windows when she smells something good cooking. Not many neighborhoods are lucky enough to share a pet horse."

Fran's words spoke for everyone: for neighbors who didn't have to mow their lawns because Bayberry's nibbling kept them trim, for children who would miss her every day at the bus stop, and hanging out with her after school.

No one had much to say after Fran finished speaking. The neighbors whispered goodbyes to Peggy and Dick, and Bayberry got a hug from everyone.

Standing alone in their driveway, Dick put his arm around Peggy's shoulders to comfort her. Bayberry walked up behind them, nudged them apart, and stood between them. They watched the neighbors disappear as the voices of the children's last goodbyes faded away.

Breaking the silence, Dick clapped his hands. "Okay, girls, let's head for New Hampshire."

Peggy gave Bayberry another piece of the clover garland. She didn't resist being led up the ramp to her trailer.

During the trip Dick stopped to allow Bayberry to walk and stretch her legs.

"Whew, this feels better than that swaying trailer," thought Bayberry.

Hours later, as the station wagon whined pulling the trailer up the hill to Cloudland Farm, Bayberry pawed the floor. She was impatient to get out.

At the top of the hill, the trailer swayed as Dick made a sharp right turn. Still climbing, he drove up the lane and stopped at the stable. The sudden stop jolted Bayberry forward, and she whinnied loudly.

"It's all right, Babe," said Peggy, opening the trailer door. She released the restraining chains before Dick lowered the rump bar and put down the ramp.

Bayberry's legs felt wobbly as she walked down the ramp. She blinked in the brightness of the afternoon sun, then she hung her head and stared at the ground, thinking, "I don't want to see where I am."

"Welcome to Cloudland Farm," called Jake's voice coming from the stable. He was carrying a pail of water.

Bayberry's ears perked slightly when she heard the strange voice. After sneaking a peek at Jake, she stared at the ground again.

"I don't want to see him, either."

5

Ruby was watching from behind the screen door as Jake walked up the hill with Peggy, Dick, and Bayberry.

"Good heavens! I hope that horse doesn't go in my gardens. Why didn't Jake put her in the stable?" she wondered.

Jake ran ahead to talk to her. "Ruby, get the carrots you bought for Bayberry. I'll stay outside with her while you have tea with the Blakes."

Ruby returned with the carrots. Jake introduced her to Peggy and Dick through the screen door.

"Come in. Come in before the black flies do," Ruby said, thrusting the carrots at Jake. "Make sure the horse eats these and not my flowers!"

Peggy couldn't believe such a tiny woman could speak with such authority.

"Sit down, sit down," commanded Ruby, pulling out chairs from the kitchen table. They sat down. Everything sparkled in Ruby's kitchen. A blue and white porcelain tea set was carefully placed on a buttercup yellow tablecloth. At the center of the table a bouquet of yellow tulips splayed from a blue crystal bowl. A large wall clock ticked and tocked as Ruby poured steaming tea into their cups and brought a plate of cookies to the table.

"Did you make these cookies?" asked Dick. Ruby's expression was no less subtle than her answer. "They don't look store-bought, do they?"

Peggy was quick to save Dick from further embarrassment by changing the subject.

"Ruby, your gardens are charming. The sights and smells walking up the hill brought back memories of springtime on my grandparents' farm."

Ruby brightened visibly, and as she and Peggy engaged in garden talk, Dick kept eating cookies.

Outside, Jake was trying to talk to Bayberry. Bayberry wasn't looking at Jake. Her eyes were on the carrots.

"Okay, Bayberry. Carrots first, and I'll talk to you later."

Watching Bayberry chewing the carrots, Jake worried that

Peggy and Dick might mention to Ruby that he had agreed to allow Bayberry to graze outside the fenced areas on Cloudland Farm as she had been trusted to do for many years in Connecticut.

Jake walked around the old horse, inspecting her.

"I can understand why you were Hunter Champion of Connecticut, Bayberry. For an old gal of twenty-seven, you have strong-looking muscles."

The only signs of Bayberry's age that Jake could see were a sway back and a cloudy-looking left eye.

Jake walked to her right side where she could see him well.

"Bayberry, a champion like you deserves happy days in old age. I'm going to do my darndest to see that you get them on Cloudland Farm."

Bayberry nickered softly. Jake felt certain she understood what he was saying to her.

The screen door opened, and Ruby looked unusually animated as she and Peggy walked to the herb garden, chatting.

Jake was relieved to see Ruby enjoying Peggy's company. "They didn't tell her about our agreement," he thought.

Dick was rubbing his stomach. Groaning, he confessed that he had eaten too many of Ruby's cookies.

Jake chuckled. "You aren't the first visitor to do that!"

Stroking Bayberry's withers, Dick looked fondly at his horse. "How did you and Bayberry get along?"

"The carrots were of more interest to her than I was."

Dick looked sadly down the hill at their station wagon with Bayberry's trailer hitched to it. "It's going to be difficult for Peggy to leave Bayberry here, Jake."

Jake put his hand on Dick's shoulder. "It's going to be hard for you, too, Dick."

"Yeah, it is."

Peggy was carrying a bouquet of herbs when she and Ruby came back from the garden. Bayberry trotted to Peggy, sniffing the herbs.

"No, girl, these are for cooking, not for you," she said, holding them behind her back.

"Come with me, Bayberry," said Jake. "I have some goodies for you."

Peggy and Dick thanked Ruby for her hospitality and followed Jake and Bayberry down the hill.

Nearing the stable, Jake took hold of Bayberry's halter to lead her inside. Bayberry whinnied loudly and balked.

Thinking quickly, Peggy held the bouquet of herbs close to Bayberry's nose and started walking backwards into the stable. Bayberry followed her, sniffing the herbs all the way into her stall.

Dick followed them into Bayberry's new stall and closed the door behind him.

After chewing a small clump of the herbs that Peggy shared with her, Bayberry lowered her head for a cool drink from her watering trough.

Dick patted her rump. "Have a good night, Bayberry. I'll come see you tomorrow."

Dick left hastily, not trying to say anymore.

Peggy put her arms around Bayberry's neck and leaned her head against her horse.

"I have to go now, too, girl, but I'll be back very early tomorrow morning with some apples, and we will go for a long trail ride together. Okay?"

Bayberry nickered softly.

"See you in the morning, Babe," Peggy said cheerfully, turning away from her horse to hide her tears.

Bayberry stretched her neck over the stall door and watched Peggy running from the stable. She heard Dick start the station wagon's motor. She whinnied mournfully, trying to call them back.

Peggy and Dick drove down the lane, pulling her empty trailer behind them.

6

Bayberry didn't know she was being watched. Beau was peering down on her stall from the loft above.

"That poor horse looks miserable. I'd better go down there and cheer her up."

Beau approached Bayberry's stall cautiously. Not wanting to frighten her, he meowed loudly before hopping on her stall door.

Three cats had lived in her Connecticut barn with her, so Bayberry was not afraid of Beau. Her ears perked toward him in curiosity.

"Hey, you aren't as droopy looking as I thought you were," said Beau.

Bayberry felt like telling him he was being sassy to talk to a stranger like that, but she was too shy to speak.

"But, I know how you feel," said Beau. "Man, I was freaked out, too, when Miki and his mom left me here. By the way, I overheard your name, Bayberry. I'm Beau, the friendly barn cat of Cloudland Farm."

Bayberry's curiosity gave her the courage to speak. "Did your family leave you here because they moved where there wasn't a barn for you to be a barn cat in?"

"No, I wasn't a barn cat 'til I came here. I was a family pet," said Beau sadly.

"That's what I was, too," said Bayberry. "I was a family pet and a neighborhood pet, too."

"Hmmm, impressive. But I bet you didn't live in a house and sleep on a bed like I did with Miki."

"No, but I had a special barn just for me with three cats who kept the mice away."

Beau shivered. He didn't want to talk about cats and mice. No way.

"Why did your family leave you here, Bayberry?"

"Because they moved where there wasn't a barn for me."

"Why can't they build a barn for you?"

"Because barns aren't allowed there." Bayberry started looking sad again.

"Hey, don't go flipping out again, Bayberry."

Bayberry lifted her head and looked at Beau. "Why did your family leave you here?"

"Because Miki was allergic to me. I gave him asthma."

"I have asthma too."

"Uh, oh, I'd better get out of here before you start wheezing." Beau was disappointed. He had thought that maybe he and Bayberry could become friends.

"No, no, I'm not allergic to cats. I'm allergic to hay. That's why Jake made a special door to the paddock for me so I can go outside to eat fresh grass whenever I want. If I eat hay, I get sick."

"Weird, a horse who can't eat hay," thought Beau.

"Well, nice talking to you, Bayberry, but I had better blow this stall before Jake catches me loafing. I'll come back later after Jake goes home for the night. I'm off on the hunt!"

Bayberry didn't like to think about what Beau had to do: catch mice. She hoped there wouldn't be any mice near her stall. She never saw them in her Connecticut barn. Their barn cats had kept them away from her.

"I hope Beau can keep the mice away from me here, but he has to do it all by himself. Can he do that?" she wondered.

That evening, after finishing his chores, Jake left the horses eating their suppers while he climbed the hill to see what Ruby had cooked for his.

Now that it was getting dark, Bayberry was growing anxious. She didn't feel like eating. "I wish Beau would come back," she said to herself.

Her ears were perked, hoping to hear Beau's meow. Instead, she heard the loud squeaking of a mouse. Her ears flickered in all directions as she searched the floor of her stall.

Seconds later Beau hopped on her door.

"Whoa, what's happening, Bayberry?"

"Mice. I'm terrified of mice. I just heard one close by."

"Relax, Boob. Now that I'm here you needn't worry, 'cuz where I am, the mice ain't. They are terrified of me. I'll stay here all night if you would like me to."

"Really?"

"Really. But we have a problem. Where will I sack out?"

"I know. You can sleep on my bedding. I don't like to lie down. It hurts me to get up. So I usually sleep standing up."

"No, thanks, those shavings look too scratchy. I'm used to soft hay. Brrr! It's chillier down here, too. It's nice and warm up in the loft."

Bayberry looked all around her stall for a suitable bed for Beau. The shavings, feed bucket, water trough, and the bare floor were all she had to offer. Except . . . except . . . No, she was too embarrassed to suggest such a thing.

"I suppose I can perch up here on your stall door," said Beau, "but it won't be very comfortable. I'm not sure I can stand it all night, Bayberry."

The frightened horse had a choice. She could be selfish and let Beau sleep on the stall door, or she could tell him her other idea.

"Beau?"

"Yeah?"

"Maybe, maybe you could sleep on my back."

"Wh-a-a-a-t? Are you crazy? I've never been on a horse's back before!"

"Well, I've never had a cat on my back before, either."

Beau's eyes narrowed as he took a closer look at his new friend's back.

"Hmmm, that little dip in the middle looks just right for me to curl up in."

"Okay, Bayberry. I suppose we can give it a try. Here goes."

Beau jumped from the door to Bayberry's back, being careful to keep his claws closed. He turned around and around before curling up in a ball. "Man, this is all right," he thought.

Bayberry liked feeling the warmth of Beau on her back. It felt good having him there. A few quiet minutes passed, and Beau fell asleep.

Bayberry lowered her head to her grain bucket. A thought crossed her mind, and her head popped up, waking Beau. "Oh no! Oh no!"

"What is the matter now, Bayberry?"

"Beau, how can you stay with me? Don't you have to hunt all night?"

"Bayberry, don't you worry about how I do my job, okay? I'm sleeping here all night."

"Thank you. Thank you, Beau."

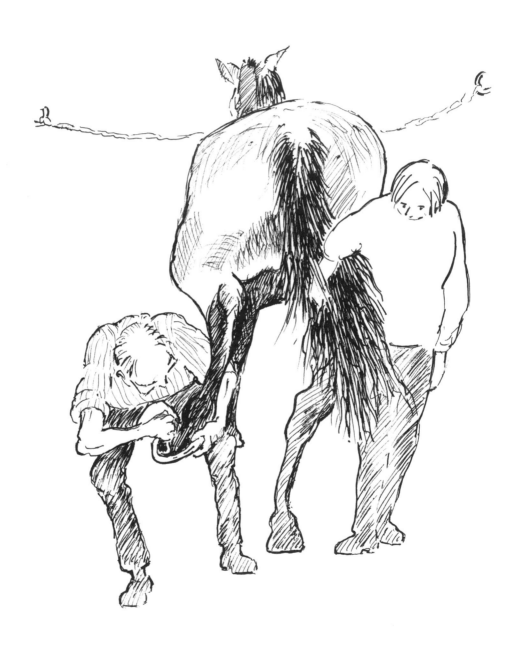

CHAPTER

7

Peggy had slept less than Bayberry on her first night in New Hampshire. She was happy to see morning come so she could drive to Cloudland Farm to let Bayberry know she and Dick had not gone back to Connecticut without her.

She left Dick sleeping, pulled on her jeans and a sweatshirt, ate a quick breakfast, and headed for Cloudland Farm.

It was a beautiful morning. The farms and fields she drove by looked their best in the freshness of early summer. Sunlight on the swaying treetops made them look more golden than green.

Driving up the hill to Cloudland Farm, she noticed ripening wild strawberries on both sides of the lane.

"Uh, oh," she thought, "those will be tempting treats for

Bayberry. She needs to be taught not to come down the lane. It's too close to the main road."

Peggy arrived at the stable as Jake was walking down from the farmhouse.

"You're an early bird, Peggy."

"I apologize for coming so early, Jake. I'm anxious to know how Bayberry is."

"Of course you are. I was, too, so I came down very early this morning to check on her, and there was quite a surprise waiting for me."

"Surprise? Is Bayberry all right?"

"Oh, yes. She's great. Follow me. She and her new friend are in the back pasture."

Peggy followed Jake through the stable and out the back door, which opened onto a beautiful meadow.

Peggy's hand covered her mouth as she gasped in surprise. In the middle of a patch of purplish-pink heads of clover stood Bayberry with a large tabby cat sitting upright on her shoulders.

"I told you you'd be surprised, Peggy."

"Is that your cat, Jake?"

"It certainly is. That is Beau, our barn cat. I knew he was lazy, but I have never seen him hitch a ride on a horse before," he said, laughing.

"None of our Connecticut cats ever went near Bayberry."

"And Beau has never gone near any of our horses."

"Jake, I need to get a picture for my daughter Wendy. She will not believe it. My camera's in my wagon."

When Peggy came back, Beau was no longer sitting up but was stretched across Bayberry. He looked like a fur collar slipped across her shoulders.

Peggy walked closer to get a better picture, but Beau jumped to the ground and ran ahead of Bayberry, who nickered softly, then trotted toward Peggy. Bayberry nuzzled Peggy, and Beau rubbed against her legs.

Peggy bent down and patted the cat. "Thanks for taking such good care of Bayberry, Beau. Tomorrow I'll bring a treat for you, too."

"Doc Pringle will be here at nine o'clock to examine Bayberry, Peggy," said Jake.

"Good. That gives me time to start teaching Bayberry where she will not be allowed to graze. I want to teach her not to go down the lane that leads to the main road. Those wild strawberries will tempt her."

"And be sure to teach her that the orchard and gardens are forbidden, too, Peggy," warned Jake. "I have assured Ruby that Bayberry can be trusted to graze outside the fences once she learns the boundaries."

Jake headed for the feed room with Beau following closely at his heels. Jake picked him up tenderly before dishing out some cat food. "Beau, if you don't start catching some mice, Ruby is going to send you away. When this bag is gone, I'm not buying any more. I hope you understand." Jake filled Beau's tin pie plate and left to feed the horses.

Dr. Pringle arrived precisely at nine o'clock. Peggy was surprised to see how old he was. He looked too frail to take care of horses.

He was very thin with white hair and a white goatee. However, when he introduced himself, his voice was strong, and his eyes were bright and friendly.

"So this is the famous Bayberry."

Bayberry's ears pointed in curiosity at the strange man staring at her, humming and pulling on his goatee.

"How old's your horse?"

"Twenty-seven," answered Peggy.

"Let's see, twenty-seven times three is eighty-one. Ha, ha! By golly, Bayberry, you and I are the same age."

Humming loudly, he started circling around the horse. When he wasn't humming and walking, he pulled on his goatee and clicked his tongue on the roof of his mouth. He removed an instrument from his bag and looked into Bayberry's eyes.

"That left eye's not much use to her, is it?"

"No. She lost her sight in it seven years ago."

"Right one does the job pretty well, does it?"

"Yes, but I worry about her stepping in holes that she can't see on her left side."

"That's a worry even when both eyes are working. Yup, always a worry."

Dr. Pringle circled Bayberry several more times.

"By golly, these legs are pretty sturdy for an old gal like you, Bayberry." He lifted her legs and scraped her hooves.

Finishing his exam and snapping his bag closed, Dr. Pringle stroked the horse's mane. "Bayberry, I'd say you were hanging in there just about the way I am. As the song goes, 'We ain't what we used to be.' But we can still enjoy a beautiful day like today, can't we?"

"I know about Bayberry's allergy to hay, Peggy. Is there anything else I should know?"

"No, I don't think so, Dr. Pringle."

"I'll go tell Jake that Bayberry passed her entrance exam with flying colors. Nice meeting you, Peggy. I expect I'll see more of you around here. Your horse is a honey."

"Thank you, Dr. Pringle. Oh, that reminds me. The barn cat seems to think so, too. This morning Jake found him sitting on

Bayberry's back."

"Beau was on Bayberry's back?"

"Yes. Have you ever seen a cat on a horse's back?"

"Nope. Can't say that I have. However, I've never known a cat that didn't hunt, either. Beau is not an ordinary cat, Peggy."

"And Bayberry is not an ordinary horse, Dr. Pringle."

8

After Peggy left, Beau found Bayberry in the paddock.

"Come on, Bayberry, let's go to the hay meadow, where the grazing is better for you."

"No, I can't go there until Peggy shows me where the holes are."

"What holes?" asked Beau.

"The ones rabbits and woodchucks make."

"Can't you see them yourself?"

Bayberry hesitated. She was embarrassed to tell Beau about her left eye. "Not very well. Not on my left side."

"Hmmm. That eye does look different. But listen, I can show you where the holes are. I have sharp eyes."

"No," protested Bayberry. "That's too much trouble for you, Beau."

"Hey, it's no big deal. If I get tired walking, I'll ride on your back. I'll be able to spot the holes better from up there, I bet. Come on."

Beau walked ahead of Bayberry in the meadow, his nose close to the ground, his eyes searching for holes.

"Stop, Bayberry. Wait here until I make sure it's safe for you to follow me."

Bayberry watched her new friend crawling carefully, sniffing the meadow floor.

"All clear, no holes here," called Beau.

Bayberry trotted to Beau and started nibbling in a patch of clover.

While Bayberry was eating, Beau, sniffing around, found a small hole that he hadn't seen at first. He lay down beside it to warn Bayberry if she walked toward it.

Neither the horse nor the cat noticed Sure Bett watching them from a far corner of the meadow.

As she watched, Bett said to herself, "Ha, this is my chance to get even with Beau. That lazy cat will fall asleep. If I walk slowly and quietly, I can sneak up and stomp on his tail. Hee, hee! Maybe Marvin will come to his rescue."

Sure Bett started walking very slowly, her ears laid back, her head lowered and stretched toward the cat and the horse. As she got closer, she could see that Beau was sleeping. But Bayberry, a wise horse with many years of experience, sensed danger. She stopped grazing and looked up to see Sure Bett coming toward them.

"Wake up, Beau! Sure Bett's getting ready to charge us!" Bayberry let out a warning squeal. Her tail was swishing angrily. She stomped on the ground.

Beau lifted his head, still sleepy. With lightning speed Bett was upon him before he could move, stepping on his tail with her right front hoof.

"I told you I would get even with you, Beau," Bett said through her clenched teeth. Bayberry pawed the ground again.

Sure Bett looked at the aged horse who was ready to do battle in Beau's defense.

"No, Bayberry, I don't want to fight with you," Bett said, lifting her hoof off Beau's tail and looking down on him.

"From now on, keep your nose out of my business, Beau." Sure Bett snorted and trotted off.

Hurrying to Beau, Bayberry asked anxiously, "Beau, Beau, are you all right?"

Beau was licking his tail. He looked up. "Yup, I'm fine, Bayberry."

"But you didn't make a sound when she was stepping on your tail. I thought you were really hurt."

"Bett's hoof wasn't hurting me 'cuz I was covering a rabbit hole with my tail so you wouldn't step in it. Bett's hoof just poked it down into the hole, so it didn't hurt very much. Just a little bit. You finish your clover, Bayberry. Sure Bett's not going to ruin our day."

Beau took a running leap, landed in the sway of Bayberry's back, and then crept to the top of her shoulders.

"Man, what a view from here, Bayberry. I'm so close to the sky I could cuff the clouds."

Dr. Pringle came back to the stable to start teaching Bayberry where she was not allowed to graze outside the fenced area. He found Bayberry and Beau in the pasture.

When Beau saw Dr. Pringle, he jumped to the ground and ran to him. Kneeling down to pet him, the old veterinarian praised the purring cat.

"You are taking good care of Bayberry, fella. Today I want you to help me teach her some lessons that will keep her safe and out of trouble."

Beau cocked his head, listening.

"I know that cat understands what I'm saying to him," thought Dr. Pringle.

Bayberry pushed her head between Beau and Dr. Pringle's hand. She sniffed at the small crop attached to a loop on his wrist.

"You remember what this is for, don't you, girl? I won't hurt you with it. I just need to teach you where you are not allowed to go around here. We want you to be safe, and we don't want you to get into trouble with Ruby."

Bayberry and Beau followed him through the gate to the yard by the stable. As Peggy had warned, the strawberries were ripening, and Bayberry had to learn that she was never to walk down the lane that led to the busy main road.

Dr. Pringle started walking toward the lane. When Bayberry followed, he flicked the crop gently on her rump. She stopped immediately. Then, very loudly, he said over and over, "No! No! No! No! No!" Then he turned her around and led her toward the farmhouse.

The next temptation was the vegetable garden, where tender shoots were beginning to appear. Bayberry sniffed and headed for it.

"No, no, Bayberry," warned Dr. Pringle. He flicked the crop on her hindquarters again. Bayberry stopped immediately. "Good girl! Good girl!"

Beau, who had been walking behind them, jumped up on Bayberry's back, sniffing where the crop had fallen on her hide. Dr. Pringle shook his head in wonderment. "I'm not hurting Bayberry, Beau."

Passing the orchard, where Ruby had planted dwarf fruit trees, Bayberry stopped and sniffed again.

"No, Bayberry, no!" said Dr. Pringle loudly.

No crop was needed this time. Bayberry knew she should not go there, either.

"Bayberry, you learn very fast. No more lessons for today. Now I'll show you a special place where you are allowed to go."

Dr. Pringle led Bayberry and Beau from the orchard around the back of the farmhouse. Below, a lush green meadow, filled with white daisies and purple clover, slanted toward trees beyond.

"That meadow is all yours, Bayberry. The other horses can't graze there because it has no fences. You and Beau go check it out. I'm going to sit up here and rest."

Dr. Pringle sat on a lawn chair next to the house. He pulled a doughnut from his pocket and looked across the meadow. Beau was walking ahead of Bayberry on her left side, his nose close to the ground.

"By golly," thought Dr. Pringle, "Beau is looking for holes."

9

Beau was exhausted after the training session with Dr. Pringle and Bayberry. He climbed to the loft to catch a nap, and soon the weary cat was having a bad dream.

In his dream, Ruby had sent him far, far away because he wasn't getting rid of the multiplying mice. He dreamed he was living in a very cold barn all by himself. The screeching wind was blowing snow through the wide cracks in the walls, and there was no hay to lie in to keep warm. He missed Miki, and Bayberry, and Jake. No one knew where to find him. He was all alone.

Jake's hammering below awakened him. He was glad to be awake. He shivered, trying to shake off his bad dream.

"Ruby can't send me away. She can't. This is where I live.

I need to take care of Bayberry." Then Beau remembered Jake's warning.

"Beau, if you don't start hunting instead of sleeping all the time, Ruby's going to send you away and get another barn cat." That thought started Beau shivering again.

Beau was so miserable he flopped flat on the floor on his stomach, feeling very sorry for himself. He stretched his front paws out and rested his head between them. This was his thinking position. His tail twitched with agitation.

"I'm not a hunter. I'm a pet. I don't want to hunt. But—but I don't want Ruby to send me away. I need to take care of Bayberry. I want to play with Miki. Nothing could be worse than never seeing Miki and Bayberry again. Nothing—not even—not even catching a mouse."

Beau stretched and sat up. He looked at his big paws and stuck out his sharp claws.

"Maybe, maybe if I can just catch one mouse a month, Ruby will think I'm doing my job, and then she won't send me away." Beau thought about his idea for a few minutes, then sitting up, he said to himself, "Yup, by golly, that's what I'll do."

Beau climbed down from the loft and ran to the feed room, where the mice came to eat the grain Jake always spilled while filling the horses' buckets. Beau remembered seeing a small hole in the wall. He would wait there.

The feed room was quiet except for the buzz of a bee on the cobwebbed window. Beau was glad to see there was grain on the floor by the metal container.

As he waited, he tried to remember how the neighbors' cats caught birds around the bird feeders at Miki's house. He crouched just the way they did so he could pounce, then strike with his paw.

Beau crouched and waited. It was boring just waiting for a mouse to come out of the hole, so he decided to practice his pounce.

He crouched, and stuck his paw way out to strike fast, but his back legs didn't spring, and he belly flopped, bumping his chin on the cement floor. He lay there feeling woozy. "I can't do it. I don't know how to pounce," he thought.

"But I have to pounce. I have to catch a mouse."

Beau crept slowly along the floor, his eyes gleaming. He crouched and waited, and waited, and waited. His back started to ache. Oh, I need to stretch. He stretched, and his head was even closer to the hole. He could now hear strange sounds coming from inside.

"Hmmm. Sounds a little bit like laughing. I'll close my eyes and pretend to be asleep, and when a mouse comes out, I'll grab it in my claws."

Near the opening, Marvin was lying on his back, kicking his tiny feet in the air, rolling from side to side.

The funny sounds grew louder. "What's that noise in there?" Beau asked.

"We're laughing," Marvin called from the hole.

"What's so funny?"

"You, Beau. You looked silly when you belly flopped." Loud laughter poured from the mouse hole.

This made Beau so angry that he thrust his paw into the hole and dragged Marvin into the feed room.

"Ouch! Your claws are digging into me, Beau."

Beau pulled in his claws but left his paw firmly planted on Marvin.

"Marvin, you mice won't be laughing long. Either I do my job catching you, or Ruby will send me away and get another cat who will."

Marvin was suddenly afraid. Beau looked huge towering over him.

"Are you going to get rid of me first, Beau?"

Beau didn't answer Marvin. He was staring at the mouse's tail, still not completely healed. He was remembering the day he rescued him from Sure Bett's stall.

"It's no use," thought Beau. "I can't hurt Marvin."

Beau slowly lifted his paw, freeing Marvin. Marvin did not run to the safety of the hole. Instead, he placed his tiny foot on top of Beau's paws.

"Beau, you are brave to let me go."

"No—no, Marvin. I'm not brave. Go back to Mattie before I change my mind."

"Beau, I'm going to organize a mouse meeting to see if we can come up with a plan to keep you here. In the meantime, we'll try to keep out of sight when Ruby comes to the stable."

Beau watched Marvin scamper back to his hole. Then he ran to the loft to do some serious thinking. Flopping on the floor, he wondered, "Can the mice really think of a way to keep Ruby from sending me away?"

10

Beau stretched out in his thinking position. He knew now that he could never hurt the mice, not even one a month.

He thought about prancing by Ruby and Jake with a mouse in his mouth.

"That's a good idea," he thought. "But how can I do that without killing the mouse?"

Beau thought about Marvin and what a good friend he had become. He wondered if the mice would think of a plan at their meeting that would save them and keep him on Cloudland Farm as the barn cat.

Beau closed his eyes and was almost asleep when an idea suddenly came to him.

"Maybe—maybe a mouse could just pretend to be dead.

He could crawl into my mouth, close his eyes, and I would make sure either Jake or Ruby saw me carrying him. Then I could run off where they couldn't see me, and I'd let the mouse go."

Beau couldn't wait to share his idea with Marvin. He ran down the ladder and streaked to the feed room. "Marvin, Marvin, I need to talk with you." Marvin came running from the hole to hear what Beau had to say.

After Beau finished explaining his idea to him, Marvin said, "Beau, that's a great idea, and you can practice on me first."

"It's a deal, Marvin."

Later, when night was falling and it was chilly in the paddock, Bayberry didn't want to go inside until Beau came back. She was dreading the night. Jake and Dr. Pringle had moved Sure Bett to her end of the stable. Now Sure Bett's stall was across from hers.

Bayberry was upset with Peggy for bringing all her championship ribbons, plaques, and pictures to Jake. He had hung them outside her stall that afternoon, and Bayberry was embarrassed. She knew Sure Bett would be jealous.

Bayberry tried to nap, but it started to rain, so she decided to go inside.

She was surprised to find Beau perched on her stall door.

"Oh, Bayberry," he said, "we have been looking at all your trophies. You were a famous champion, weren't you?"

"That was a long time ago, Beau."

"How old are you?" asked Sure Bett crisply.

"Twenty-seven."

"I'm going to be a champion, too," bragged Bett.

"I believe you will be, Bett," said Bayberry. "Your trainer Tillie will help you become one if you work hard."

"I don't need that bossy Tillie to become a champion."

"You aren't a champion unless you win in horse shows. You can't do that alone—unless you can ride yourself!" Beau chuckled to himself.

"I don't pay any attention to all that stuff Tillie tells me. I'm tired of her making me do silly things," muttered Sure Bett.

"If you don't listen to her, you'll never be a champion, Bett."

"Just because you are old, don't start giving me advice, Bayberry."

"You need advice, Bett. You are a mean mare. You try to make everyone as miserable as you are. Now please be quiet. I need to go sleep."

Beau was proud of Bayberry for giving Bett good advice, he whispered to her. "I have good news, Bayberry. Follow me to the paddock so we can talk."

Outside, Beau perched on the rail fence. Bayberry stood close to him, eager to hear his news.

"Today I had a bad dream up in the loft, Bayberry. A very bad dream. Ruby had sent me far away to a cold and lonely barn because I wasn't doing my job as the barn cat here."

Beau paused. "You know my secret, don't you, Bayberry?" Bayberry didn't answer him.

"You do. I know you do."

"Well, I know you don't like to hunt. But the mice are afraid of you. They don't know you won't catch them."

"Yes, they do, Bayberry."

"They do? Oh, dear, now they will come creeping into my stall."

"No, they won't. Definitely not. Trust me, Bayberry. They will never come near you. I made a deal with them. We have a plan that will keep them safe and also keep Ruby from sending me away. I'll explain it to you tomorrow."

"Will you come back in the morning?"

"Yup, I'll meet you in the paddock. This has been a long day. Cheerio, Bayberrio!"

Beau felt like creeping to the loft, but he hurried to the feed room to keep his date with Marvin.

Peeking into the hole, Beau called to him, "Psst, Marvin, I'm ready to practice with you!"

Marvin poked his head out and crawled reluctantly out of his hole.

"Let's practice outside the feed room, Beau. I don't want the other mice watching us."

"Okay."

Near the stable door, Beau crouched down and opened his mouth wide.

Marvin looked at Beau's gaping mouth and his long fangs.

He shuddered. "Those long teeth will stab me."

"Just crawl in behind them, Marvin. I only have them in the front of my mouth. I won't close my jaws all the way, and those stubby teeth in back of the sharp ones won't hurt you."

Beau opened his mouth, and Marvin crawled in. He lay down with his head sticking out one side of Beau's half-closed mouth, and his tail out the other.

Beau took a few steps. Marvin yelled, "Drop me, drop me!"

Beau spit him out. Poor Marvin looked wet and miserable as he landed on the floor.

"Did I hurt you, Marvin?"

"No, but I don't like your rough tongue rubbing my face."

"I'll try to hold it up. Let's try it one more time."

Poor Marvin, being an agreeable mouse, crawled back into Beau's mouth.

The cat started high stepping, practicing his proud prance, when suddenly the stable door slid open.

Terrified by the sudden noise, Marvin jumped from Beau's mouth and streaked to his hole. Beau ran after him, pretending he was chasing him.

A very surprised and happy Jake followed Beau into the feed room, where the cat was crouching by the mouse hole.

"Good boy, Beau! Good boy. Wait until I tell Ruby!"

11

The smell of French toast cooking awakened Miki. He ran to the kitchen. "Is today Saturday, Mom?"

"It certainly is. Uncle Jake called early this morning to make sure we were coming. He can't wait for you to meet Beau's new friend."

"What new friend?"

"I don't know, dear. He said you would be surprised, but he didn't say why."

"Will Beau be playing with his new friend, or will he still play with me?"

"Well of course he will play with you. Why wouldn't he?"

"Probably if his new friend can pick him up and scratch his ears, he'll like him better than me."

"Beau will never like anyone better than you, silly. But you wouldn't want him to have just one friend, would you?"

"No," said Miki softly.

"You have lots of other friends, dear."

"But I only have one pet, Mom."

"I know, dear, and Beau misses you as much as you miss him."

Later, driving to Cloudland Farm, Miki was still worried. "If Beau likes his new friend better than me, I don't want to stay at Uncle Jake's and play with them, Mom."

"I don't understand why you are so upset, Miki. Beau is going to be very happy to see you. It doesn't change his feelings about you just because he has another friend."

Mother's words were not reassuring to him. Miki did not talk to her the rest of the way.

When the horses saw the station wagon coming up the lane, they ran back and forth along the fence. Uncle Jake came hurrying from the stable. He lifted Miki into his arms, exclaiming how heavy he was.

"Where's Beau, Uncle Jake?"

"Oh—ho ho—wait until you meet Beau's new friend, Miki. You are going to be very surprised."

"When can I see them?"

"Soon, but first you need to change into your farm clothes.

Aunt Ruby has some cookies and milk waiting for you up at the house."

A young Appaloosa whinnied loudly, begging Miki to notice her. Sure Bett came from behind and nudged her aside.

"Miki, the horses are waiting for their carrots. I think you should give them some before we go to see Aunt Ruby."

"I don't want to right now, Mom."

"Then I will. You go along with Uncle Jake."

Miki's stomach felt funny. He didn't want any milk or cookies. He didn't want to meet Beau's friend, either. He just wanted to go home. He dreaded having to sit at the table with the grown-ups. "If Mother makes me eat, I will throw up," he thought.

Aunt Ruby was waiting for him behind the screen door. He knew she would tell him what to do. She always did.

"Are you feeling better, Miki?" she asked, opening the door for him.

"Yup."

"Good. Well, your clothes are in the laundry room. Run in there and change before you have some milk and cookies."

Pulling off his clothes in the laundry room, Miki couldn't keep from crying. He was upset that he had to wear different clothes around the animals. Why did he have to have asthma? He was mad at Aunt Ruby for being bossy.

He didn't want to meet Beau's new friend.

He could hear the grown-ups talking about boring things at the table. He didn't want to go sit with them.

"Miki, your milk's getting warm, and your cookies are getting cold." Aunt Ruby's bossy voice again.

"Mom, can you come here, please?"

Mother left the table and went quickly to see what Miki needed.

Miki was crying. "I don't feel well. I have a stomach-ache. I can't eat anything. I want to go home. I want to go home right now."

Hugging him, Mother spoke softly. "I think if you lie in the hammock for a few minutes, you will feel better, dear. Come on, let's go outside."

After settling Miki in the hammock, Mother went to explain why he wasn't coming to the table.

"I'm done with my coffee. I'll go keep the boy company," volunteered Jake.

Jake knelt by the hammock. "I'm sorry you're not feeling well, son. What's the matter?"

"My stomach aches. I want Mom to take me home."

"Don't you feel well enough to look for Beau? I think he's in the lower pasture behind the house."

"Is his friend with him?"

"She was when I saw them earlier."

"His friend is a girl?"

"Sort of—well, yes—yes, she's a girl. Come on, son, it's high time you met her. Besides, I need you to solve the mystery."

Miki's legs felt wobbly as he climbed out of the hammock and followed Jake along the path that wound around the house. At the top of the hill, Jake shaded his eyes with his hand and scanned the meadow. "They must have gone into the alders. I don't see them."

Miki walked behind his uncle. He didn't want to look at any old girl who had taken his friend away.

"There they are, coming out of the bushes."

Miki put his hand over his eyes. When he peeked through his fingers, he saw Beau, sitting upright on Bayberry's shoulders.

"That's not a girl. That's a horse! Is Beau's friend a horse?"

"She sure is, son."

Miki flew down the hill calling, "Beau! Beau!"

The horse and cat heard him and looked up. Beau jumped down and ran toward him with Bayberry trotting behind.

Miki wanted to pick Beau up and bury his face in his soft fur, but he knew he couldn't. Beau rubbed and purred against his legs.

"You are happy to see me, aren't you, Beau?"

Bayberry nickered for attention, and when Miki looked up at her, she tried to nuzzle him.

"No, Bayberry. You can't get near Miki's face," said Uncle Jake, pulling her away from him.

"You can imagine how surprised I was, Miki, when I went down to check on Bayberry after her first night in the stable and found Beau riding on her back in the pasture."

Miki had his thinking look on his face. "Probably if Beau missed me and Bayberry missed her family, they became friends."

"You know, son, I think that is what probably happened."

Miki was so relieved that Beau's friend was a horse.

"I like Bayberry, Uncle Jake."

"She's a great horse, Miki. She is in very good shape for her age. And, guess what? She has asthma, too."

"She does?"

"Yup. Allergic to hay. The dust in it makes her cough and sneeze, just as it does you."

"Lucky she isn't allergic to cats, Uncle Jake."

"Bayberry has another problem, too, Miki. She is blind in her left eye. If she steps in a hole, she could break a leg. I keep filling holes when I find them, but they are hard to see. That's a good job for you, son. Looking for holes in the grazing area."

"Beau will help me look for them, too, Uncle Jake."

"That's a great idea, Miki."

"May I feed the horses their treats now?"

"Indeed you may."

Clapping his hands, Miki called, "Come, Beau. Come, Bayberry."

Beau jumped on Bayberry's shoulders. Jake watched Miki walking beside them up the hill. Jake beamed. "They are friends already."

12

Miki was having such a happy time with Bayberry and Beau, Ruby invited him and Mother to stay for supper. In the evening, soon after they left for home, a sudden summer storm swept over Cloudland Farm.

Bayberry was resting in her stall. She was exhausted after following Miki and Beau all afternoon, visiting their secret hiding places around Cloudland Farm.

Beau was tired, too, but he was on his way to the mouse meeting with Marvin. As he crawled behind Marvin under the stable where all the other mice were waiting for them, his heart was thumping with fear. When Beau looked upon the multitude of mice facing him, he was terrified. The mice were packed so closely together they blurred into a sea of gray dotted with tiny black eyes staring at him.

Marvin stood tall on his hind legs and began to address his audience. Beau hunched up beside him, hoping his fur wasn't rippling from his shivering.

"Fellow mice," began Marvin, "don't be afraid of my friend Beau. He is not here to harm you. He is here to save you."

"They may not be afraid of me, but I sure am of them," thought Beau, as the mice cheered and clapped their tiny feet.

"Ruby is threatening to send Beau away," continued Marvin, "because he isn't doing his job as a barn cat."

Marvin paused and cleared his throat. "We mice all know what Beau is supposed to do to us, don't we? Hmm?"

The mice looked around, nodding to one another, murmuring. "Ruby's plan is to bring a killer cat to Cloudland Farm to get rid of all of us." Marvin waved his paw in a broad gesture over the gasping mice. "But don't worry, my friends. That is not going to happen! Our friend Beau and I have a plan that will save us mice and keep Beau on Cloudland Farm."

Loud cheers erupted, and the mice all clapped so hard the horses in the stable heard them.

"What's that funny noise?" asked Bett loudly, waking

Bayberry. All the horses in the stable perked their ears, but no more sounds came from below. Marvin was calmly explaining his and Beau's plan to the mice.

Bett's and Bayberry's necks stretched over their stall doors.

Bayberry was surprised when Sure Bett started speaking softly to her.

"Bayberry, I'm sorry I frightened you in the meadow. I wasn't trying to really hurt Beau. I just wanted to teach him to keep his nose out of my business. When Marvin was stealing my grain, I was just trying to scare him, too, so he would stop coming into my stall. I don't like mice creeping and crawling around me."

"I—I don't, either, Bett. That's why Beau slept on my back before the mice promised him they would keep away from me."

Bett sighed. "Aren't you bored here, Bayberry?" she asked.

"No, Bett, I'm not. I'm old now. I can't work hard and do all the things I did with Wendy anymore. Sometimes I miss going to horseshows. I liked competing with a lot of other horses."

"Weren't you bored when Wendy made you do the same things over and over?"

"Nope. That's what it takes to win in competition. I used to get tired and frustrated, but I was never bored because Wendy was always patient and kind to me. My first owner was a mean man. He said that I would never be a champion."

"Then—then how come you became a champion, Bayberrry?"

"Because Wendy and I worked very hard, and Wendy believed in me."

That made Sure Bett think about Tillie, her trainer, who was nice to her, too.

"Bayberry?"

"Yes?"

"Do you think I can be a champion like you?"

"Oh, yes. Yes, I do, Bett."

CHAPTER

13

The next week on Cloudland Farm was busy and happy. It was Saturday morning again.

Dick and Peggy had come to see Bayberry before going away for a few days.

Beau was up early so he could finish practicing with the mice before Miki came. He was crouching by the mouse hole when Jake came into the feed room to fill the horses' grain buckets.

"So, Beau, you're up for an early breakfast, eh?"

Beau ran to him, rubbing and purring against his legs before going to the cat food cupboard.

"So, what do you want, Beau, a little cereal to go with your mouse? Okay, fella. Keep catching mice, and I'll keep buying cat food."

Tillie, Bett's trainer, had come to the stable very early that morning. She was taking Sure Bett to a large arena fifty miles away to spend the day. Tillie was so thrilled with Bett's mysterious change in attitude and hard work in the riding ring all week that she was eager to see how she would react to being with a lot of horses she didn't know.

Jake helped Tillie load Sure Bett into her trailer. As he watched them driving down the lane, he said aloud, "Oh, Bett, please be good for Tillie today."

Miki and his mother were coming at noon. Jake had a lot of errands to do before lunch. He ran up to the farmhouse for his shopping list, then hopped into his truck and headed into town.

Mother and Miki arrived before they were expected. This threw Ruby into a tizzy. She sputtered as she made room in the refrigerator for all the cheese and chicken livers they had brought for Beau.

"Hurry up and change, Miki. I want you to go out back and watch Bayberry until Jake gets back from town. He said Beau was watching her, but I don't see him down there with the horse."

"Is there anything I can do to help you?" asked Mother.

"Nope. Why don't you rest outside in the hammock while I scrub the kitchen floor?"

Mother looked at the floor that seemed clean already, but she was happy to have some idle time outside by herself.

Miki changed his clothes, then ran around the house and down to the meadow.

He saw the horse grazing, but he couldn't see Beau. Bayberry saw him and trotted toward him. Miki pulled out his gloves and patted her as he looked around for his pet.

For a while Miki looked for holes. But it was boring without Beau.

He sat down and watched Bayberry graze. "This is boring, too. Horses just eat and eat and eat. Beau is much more fun to play with."

"Here, Beau. Here, Beau."

He didn't come. Bayberry walked toward him and looked at him with her friendly eyes.

"I like you, Bayberry, but I miss Beau. Let's go find him."

Bayberry followed Miki up the hill. Ruby was on her hands and knees scrubbing the kitchen floor and didn't see them walk by the door to the hammock.

"Mom, Bayberry didn't want to stay down there without Beau. Have you seen him"?

"No, I haven't, but I don't think Bayberry should be here so close to Ruby's garden."

"I'm watching her, Mom."

"Beau's probably hunting, dear. Aunt Ruby said he's been catching lots of mice."

"You mean he's a real barn cat now and not a pet anymore?"

"He can be both, Miki. The horses in the paddock are waiting for their apples. I think you should go and feed them."

Beau was missing Miki, too. He was with Marvin, carrying the other mice. Peeking through the tall grass, he saw Miki and Mother. He didn't want them to see him. He knew he looked ridiculous with a mouse dangling from his mouth.

Beau and Marvin were having a hard time practicing with the other mice, who seemed heavier than Marvin. As each mouse crawled into Beau's mouth, Marvin tried to help balance them on Beau's tongue, but they kept falling off.

"Oh, I wish I could be with Bayberry and Miki," sighed Beau.

The horses nickered and flicked their tails in excitement when they saw Miki walking to the fence with a bag of apples, Bayberry following behind.

A light breeze was blowing, and Bayberry sniffed the air. "Mmmm, strawberries. I smell strawberries."

Without thinking where she was going, she followed the scent. Heading down the lane, she remembered the sting of the crop on her hide and Dr. Pringle yelling, "No! No! No, Bayberry!"

She looked back at Miki talking to the horses. Jake was in

town, and Ruby was talking to Miki's mother in the hammock. No one was watching her.

"I'll just walk a little way," she thought.

Bayberry sniffed her way down the lane until she saw them. There they were—a huge cluster of ripe strawberries. Bayberry lowered her head for her first bite. She closed her eyes and chewed the delicious fruit, sweet red juice filling her mouth.

"These are the sweetest strawberries I have ever tasted!"

Lowering her head for a second bite, she did not notice the opening and closing of a narrow path through the grass. A garter snake, coming toward her, slithered through the strawberry leaves and rubbed against her nose.

Startled, Bayberry squealed and shied, then took off in a full gallop down the lane toward the main road. She was too frightened to think about where she was going.

Mother and Miki heard her squealing. They ran down the lane, yelling at her to stop. Bayberry didn't hear them.

Beau, practicing in the tall grass close to the lane, also heard the squealing. He dropped the mouse in his mouth and streaked by Mother and Miki to overtake the runaway horse. He jumped onto the rail fence and then took a flying leap through the air, landing high on Bayberry's neck. Bayberry squealed and reared, and the sudden stop catapulted Beau down onto the road.

At that moment, Jake's pickup truck turned into the lane. He had to swerve into the ditch to avoid hitting the horse and cat. Jake jumped from the truck and grabbed Bayberry's halter.

Bayberry was wild with fright, and it took all of Jake's strength to get hold of her and reassure her that everything was all right.

"Okay, girl, you are okay," Jake said over and over with a calming voice.

Beau was hunched up and shivering in the lane. Miki ran to him, scooped his pet into his arms, and buried his head in his fur.

"I—I don't care if I get asthma, Mom."

"Son," yelled Jake, "bring Beau over here so Bayberry will know he's all right. Don't come too close until I get her calmed down. Just stand where she can see you and Beau."

Jake's plan worked. When Bayberry saw Beau in Miki's arms, she gradually stopped resisting Jake.

"Okay, son, come closer with Beau."

Mother was nervous, but she trusted Jake's judgment.

"Set him down, Miki."

When Beau's feet touched the ground, he shook himself, then ran to Bayberry. Bayberry lowered her head and sniffed him.

"What in the world's going on down here?" asked Ruby, hurrying toward them.

"Everything's all right, Ruby."

"What's your truck doing in the ditch?"

"I'll explain later. Right now I need to take Bayberry into the stable and calm her down."

14

Miki followed Mother and Ruby up the hill, carrying Beau in his arms. Beau's paws stretched over Miki's shoulders, and their heads pressed together. Beau's purring tickled Miki's ear, a feeling he had missed for a long time.

Miki carried Beau to a lawn chair next to the picnic table. A large maple tree spread like an umbrella above them, protecting them from the midday sun.

Beau settled down in Miki's lap. Miki stroked his butterscotch and cream-colored fur.

"Oh, Beau, I've missed you so much."

Soon they fell asleep, exhausted from the excitement of the morning.

Ruby's voice awakened them. She was unfolding a tablecloth

when she saw Jake and Bayberry coming up the hill.

"Jake, don't bring that horse up here. We're eating outside."

"Bayberry won't bother us," Jake said firmly. Ruby snapped the tablecloth in the air, smoothed it on the picnic table, and hurried back to the kitchen.

Seeing Beau and Miki, Bayberry trotted over to nuzzle them.

"Hey, Bayberry, stop that!" yelled Jake. "Miki, you shouldn't let the animals get close to your face. You'll get asthma, son."

"Mom said I could hold Beau because he was so scared. She gave me a pill so I won't get too wheezy. Bayberry was scared, too, Uncle Jake."

Mother and Ruby came from the kitchen carrying trays of sandwiches and cookies and a pitcher of lemonade. The telephone rang, and Ruby ran back in the house to answer it.

She came back soon, carrying another tray.

"Jake, that was Tillie calling. She said she and Bett are having a great day. They won't be home until quite late, and she didn't want us to worry. She said Sure Bett behaved very well with the other horses."

"That is wonderful news, Ruby."

"Bless Doc Pringle," thought Jake. "It was his idea to move Sure Bett to a stall close to Bayberry's."

"Miki," said Ruby, "I brought out Beau's cheese and chicken

livers, and some sliced apples for Bayberry. Why don't you take it over to them so we can eat our lunch in peace without begging animals staring at us?"

Miki took the tray and called Beau and Bayberry to a spot away from the picnic table. Jake watched the boy, the cat, and the horse huddled together, the animals patiently waiting for Miki to dole out the goodies.

"Miki," called Ruby. "You don't have to feed the animals. Come eat your lunch."

Miki gave Bayberry and Beau a pat before reluctantly following Ruby's order.

An uninvited guest to the picnic was hiding in the grass. Marvin was worried about Beau, and he had come to see if he was all right. After Miki left to eat, Marvin crawled closer and talked to Beau.

"Are you and Bayberry all right, Beau?"

"Yup. We're both okay, Marvin."

"Good. You guys really scared me."

"Beau, I just had an idea," Marvin continued. "Wouldn't this be a good time to prance by the picnic table with me in your mouth?"

"Man, I'm not sure I'm up to any more excitement today, Marvin."

Beau glanced over at the family sitting at the picnic table. "Well, I don't really feel like it, Marvin, but I guess you are probably right. This is a good time. But—I don't know how to begin."

"I have it all figured out," said Marvin. First, Beau, no cat catches a mouse without a good chase. So, I'll run ahead of you in the tall grass. You leap high and bound after me so they will be certain to see you. Then, you stop suddenly, jump high, and pounce. When you stop running, they will know you have caught something. That's when I will crawl into your mouth. Next, you walk out of the tall grass and prance by the picnic table proudly displaying your catch before you run off to eat me in peace, only pretending, of course! And please, Beau, don't prance too long."

"Okay, Marvin, let's get it over with. I'll see you later, Bayberry." Beau disappeared in the tall grass, following Marvin.

Miki noticed immediately that Beau was not with Bayberry, who was calmly eating her apple slices.

"I wonder where Beau went," said Miki.

"There he is," said Ruby. "He's chasing something in the tall grass."

"By golly, you're right, Ruby," said Jake. "Beau's hunting, even after eating all that cheese and liver."

A few seconds later, Mother gasped. "Here he comes with a mouse in his mouth!"

"Look at our hunter, Ruby. Isn't he something?" bragged Jake.

Ruby stared at Beau carrying Marvin in his mouth. "Now I do believe Beau's a hunter, Jake," she said, shaking her head and almost smiling.

Beau came prancing proudly toward the picnic table, with Marvin's head and tail poking out between his jaws. He walked so close to Ruby that Marvin's tail rubbed against her leg.

"Shoo, Beau! Shoo!" yelled Ruby, flailing her arms. "Don't bring that mouse over here."

Beau changed direction rapidly and disappeared in the tall grass. Out of sight, he dropped Marvin, and both of them lay panting on the ground.

"I'm glad there are a lot of other mice you can practice carrying, Beau. That's hard work!"

"Yeah, Marvin, but I'm the only cat," said Beau. "Man, I can't do this every day."

Miki had finished lunch, and he and Bayberry were anxious for Beau to come back. They were relieved when they saw the bedraggled cat coming toward them.

Beau looked so tired that Miki picked him up, stood on tiptoes, and laid him in the little dip in Bayberry's back.

"Miki," called Mother, "you need to come and rest for a while."

"Okay, Mom. I'll see you later, Bayberry and Beau."

"You must be very tired, Beau," said Bayberry when they were alone.

"You must be tired, too, Bayberry."

"I am, but I didn't have to chase a mouse."

"Or a horse!" teased Beau.

"I'm sorry, Beau. I'll never go down the lane again. I promise."

"I believe you, Bayberry. Man, I'm tired. You wander and graze wherever you please. I'm gonna sack out. It feels great to be up here, so close to the clouds."

The End

The Origins of *Bayberry & Beau*

When Nita Choukas's friends moved from Connecticut to New
Hampshire, they boarded their twenty-three-year-old quarter horse,
Bayberry, at a nearby stable. Living in Bayberry's new barn was a
handsome tabby cat.

The cat had never shown much interest in the other horses at the
stable. Bayberry had always ignored the three cats who lived in her old
barn in Connecticut. Mysteriously, the two animals bonded with each
other. Nita's friends invited her to visit and see the wonderful creatures
firsthand, and they suggested that she write about this unusual friendship.

Nita doubted she was the right person to write the story. She had
written for the theater before, but this would be something new. But
when she arrived at the farm and saw Bayberry with a cat stretched
out over her shoulders, she was inspired. Nita immediately sensed that
this could be the basis for a wonderful children's story.

As a seventy-five-year-old grandmother, writing her first book
seemed like a big challenge. It took Nita several years to think of the
right way to tell the story of these two unusual friends. Finally, the story
came together in her mind, and she teamed up with artist Gillian Tyler
to create *Bayberry & Beau*.

welcome to
chelsea green kids

Chelsea Green Publishing Company proudly introduces our new **Chelsea Green Kids** collection. We believe that a comprehensive education is more than just passing a standardized exam—it is essential that kids learn how their choices and actions impact the natural world and the other people with whom they share the planet.

Chelsea Green Kids introduces children to these concepts with fun and engaging plot lines, unforgettable characters and easy-to-use teacher/ parent guides. These upbeat books empower children to become active stewards of the Earth—they don't need to wait until they are grown-ups to make a difference.

The ZERI Fables make learning science fun. These bilingual Spanish/English books focus on specific scientific concepts while also cultivating emotional intelligence, eco-literacy, creativity, and artistic aptitude. The books include teacher/parent guides and hands-on activities to help children apply what they have learned. Illustrations by Pamela Salazar Ocampo.

The Ant Farmer
ISBN 958-692-847-0

Colombian Mushrooms
ISBN 958-692-827-6

Forest Drinking Water
ISBN 958-692-778-4

Grow a House
ISBN 958-692-773-3

The King of Hearts
ISBN 958-692-770-9

Oranges from Soap
ISBN 958-692-843-8

The Smart Mushroom
ISBN 958-692-771-7

The Strongest Tree
ISBN 958-692-838-1

Walking on Water
ISBN 958-692-781-4

Why Can't I Steal Less?
ISBN 958-692-768-7

Why Don't They Like Me?
ISBN 958-692-828-4

$9.95 | paperback | 6 ½ x 9 ½
33 pages | full color, illustrated,
Spanish and English,
for ages 5–8

Lee Welles's Gaia Girls series turns science into an adventure. In each book a girl from a different region of the world is given power over one of the four elements: earth, air, fire, and water. She must learn to use this power to help the Earth—Gaia—survive.

Gaia Girls™

Enter the Earth
Lee Welles
Illustrated by Ann Hameister

Elizabeth loves to work on her family's farm and play with her best friend, Rachel. Then Harmony Farms Corporation moves to town. Many families, including Rachel's, are selling their land and moving away. When all seems hopeless, Elizabeth meets Gaia, the living Earth. Elizabeth discovers strange powers and faces difficult responsibilities as she challenges Harmony Farms' pollution and influence.

$18.95 | hardcover | 5 ½ x 8
336 pages | ISBN 1-933609-00-1
black and white illustrations, for young adults

Nobody Particular
One Woman's Fight to Save the Bays
Molly Bang

Molly Bang's *Nobody Particular* is the true story of how Diane Wilson—who was, as she says, "nobody particular"—succeeded in forcing a huge corporation to stop polluting the bays where she made her living as a shrimper.

$10 | paper | 8 ½ x 11 | 48 pages
ISBN 1-931498-94-6 | full color throughout, for ages 11–18

CHELSEA GREEN PUBLISHING
the politics and practice of sustainable living

For more information about **Chelsea Green Kids** books or to request a catalog, go to www.chelseagreen.com, call toll-free (800) 639-4099, or write to us at P.O. Box 428, White River Junction, Vermont 05001.